"For Lauren, Dara, Walter, Osker and Markley"

First published in Great Britain 2022 by Farshore
This edition published for Scottish Book Trust in 2024 by Dean

An imprint of HarperCollins*Publishers*
1 London Bridge Street, London SE1 9GF
www.farshore.co.uk

HarperCollins*Publishers*
Macken House, 39/40 Mayor Street Upper,
Dublin 1, D01 C9W8, Ireland

Copyright © Alex Willmore 2022
Alex Willmore has asserted his moral rights.

ISBN 978 0 00 865898 4
Printed in Malaysia
001

A CIP catalogue record for this title is available from the British Library.

I DID SEE A MAMMOTH!

ALEX WILLMORE

Farshore

We're exploring the Antarctic for penguins.
But I'm going to see a MAMMOTH.

*Don't be silly! You can't see
a mammoth! And why would
you want to when you can see . . .*

FABULOUS,

CUTE,

GLORIOUS,

PENGUINS!

But I'm not here to see penguins . . .

I'm here to see a mammoth.

I'm *going* to see a . . .

LOOK! I saw a great big mammoth,
on a skateboard . . .
wearing SUNGLASSES!

Er, you can't have seen a mammoth.
Mammoths are extinct. And I'm pretty
sure they're not even from around here.

Are you certain what you saw wasn't
a wonderful, majestic, glorious penguin . . .
on a skateboard . . . wearing sunglasses?

It *wasn't* a silly penguin.
I didn't see a penguin.

I definitely, definitely, definitely saw a . . .

M.. M... M....

MAMMOTH! MAMMOTH! MAMMOTH! MAMMOTH! MAMMOTH! MAMMOTH! MAMMOTH! MAMMOTH!

I saw a mammoth!
A great big mammoth
on a skateboard,
wearing sunglasses
and a tutu
and doing BALLET!

*Oh, I'm sure it was just a wonderful skateboarding,
ballet-dancing penguin that you saw.*

Pfft.

I *did* see a mammoth.

I absolutely,
definitely saw a . . .

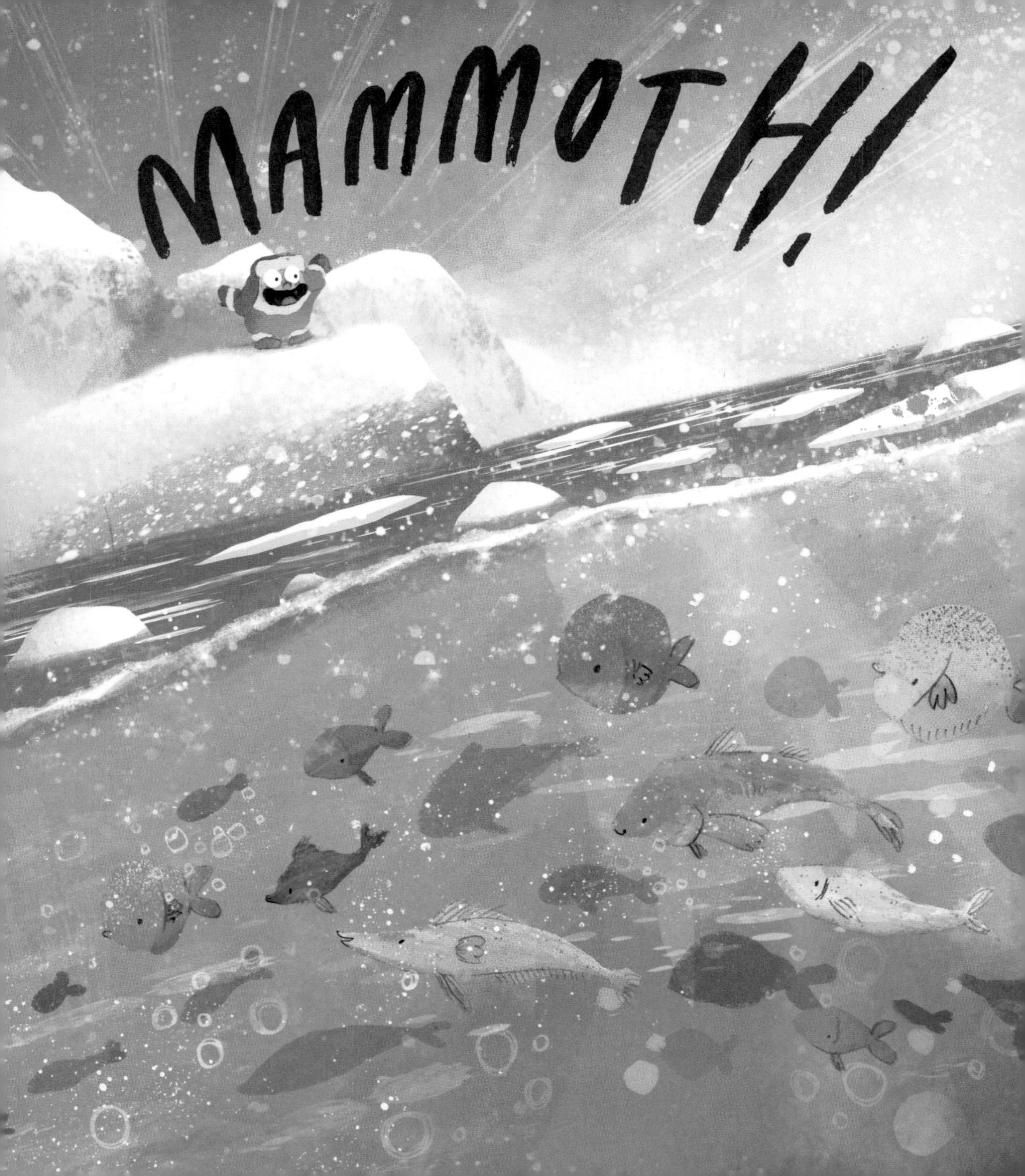
MAMMOTH!

MAMMOTH! MAMMOTH! MAMMOTH! MAMMOTH!

I SAW A GREAT BIG MAMMOTH on a SKATEBOARD, wearing SUNGLASSES and a TUTU and a TOP HAT

and also it was SWIMMING using FLIPPERS . . . AND A SNORKEL!

No . . .

you . . .

didn't!

Yes. I. DID.
I'll show you.

It's right over . . .

. . . here?!

NO!

NO!

NO! NO!

I DID SEE A

MAN

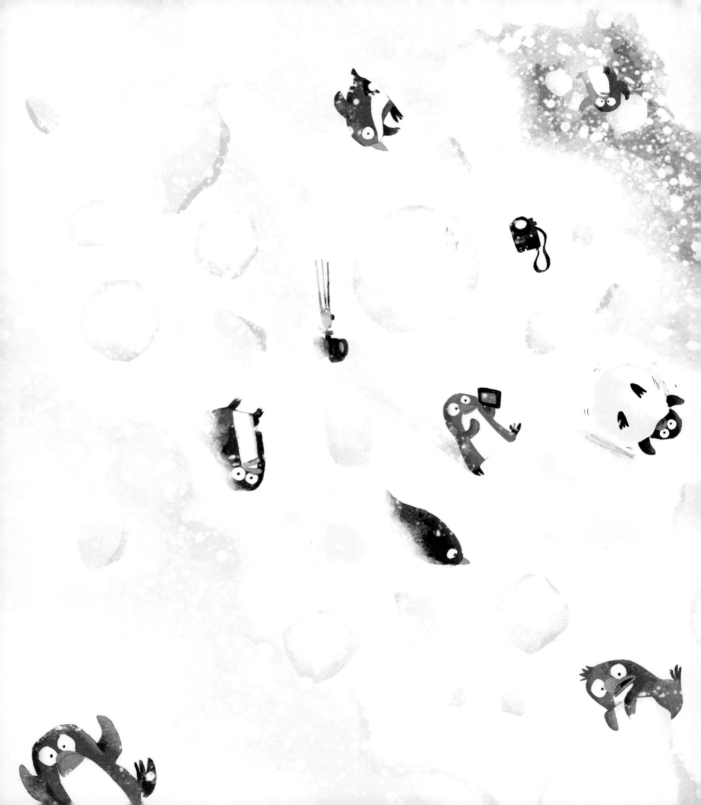

Sigh. Maybe I *didn't* see a . . .

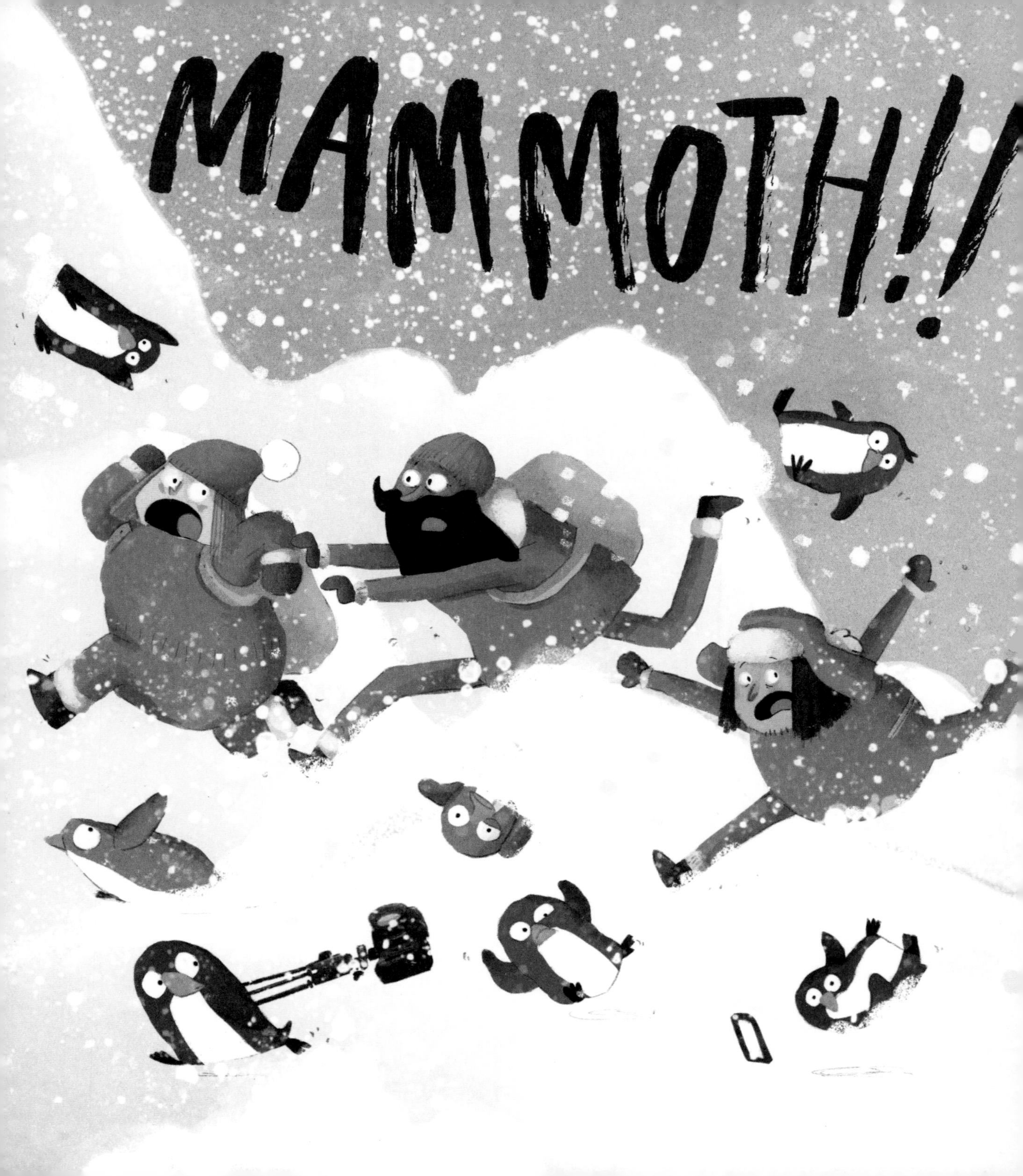
MAMMOTH!!

Woolly mammoths are ancient relatives of today's elephants.
If you'd been alive 10,000 years ago, and lived in northern Europe,
northern Asia, north America or the Arctic, you might well have
met one.

Meeting a penguin is a lot easier. The southern hemisphere is home to eighteen
different species, including five species that live or breed in Antarctica. So far,
no evidence of mammoths has been found there - but there's no harm looking!